To Mark and Lia, who bring endless
wit, wisdom, love and inspiration to my life

Book design by Susan Verlander and Sara Gillingham.
Typeset in Mrs. Eaves.
The illustrations in this book were rendered in Adobe Illustrator.
Manufactured in Singapore.

Library of Congress Cataloging-in-Publication Data
Verlander, Susan.
Goodnight, Country / by Susan Verlander.
p. cm.
Summary: Explores the sights and sounds of going to bed in the country,
from dinner bells ringing and screen doors swinging
to mice pattering and knitting needles chattering.
ISBN 0-8118-4172-3
[1. Country life—Fiction. 2. Bedtime—Fiction. 3. Stories in rhyme.]
I. Title.
PZ8.3.V71264Go 2004
[E]—dc21
2003008932

Distributed in Canada by Raincoast Books
9050 Shaughnessy Street, Vancouver, British Columbia V6P 6E5

10 9 8 7 6 5 4 3 2 1

Chronicle Books LLC
85 Second Street, San Francisco, California 94105

www.chroniclekids.com

goodnight,
country

SUSAN VERLANDER

chronicle books · san francisco

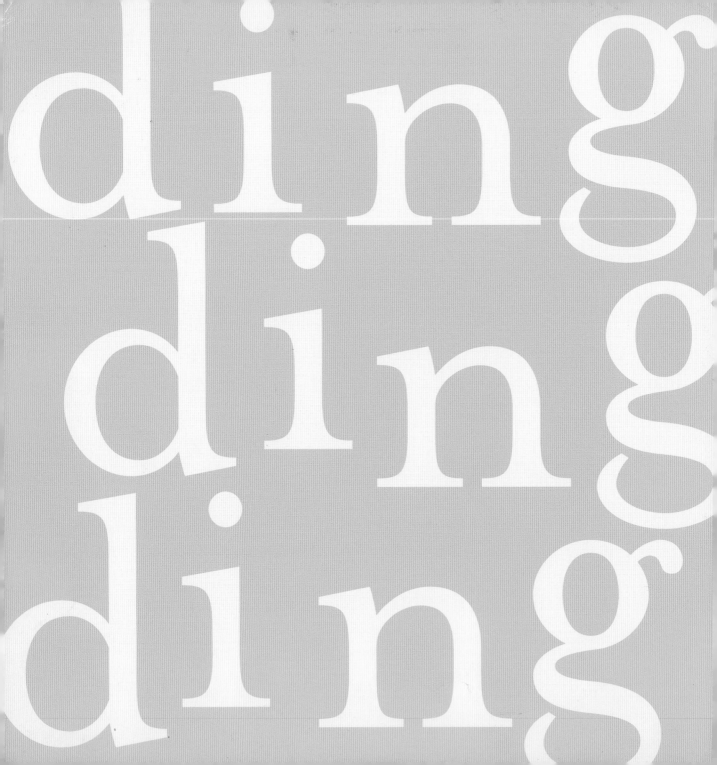

dinner bells ring

screen doors swing

farmers stop

kitchens hop

dishes clack

checkers stack

quilts bloom

fireflies zoom

potbelly glows

grandfathers doze

mice patter

knitting needles chatter

bats squeak

porch swings creak

stories charm

kisses warm

dreams appear

nighttime is here!

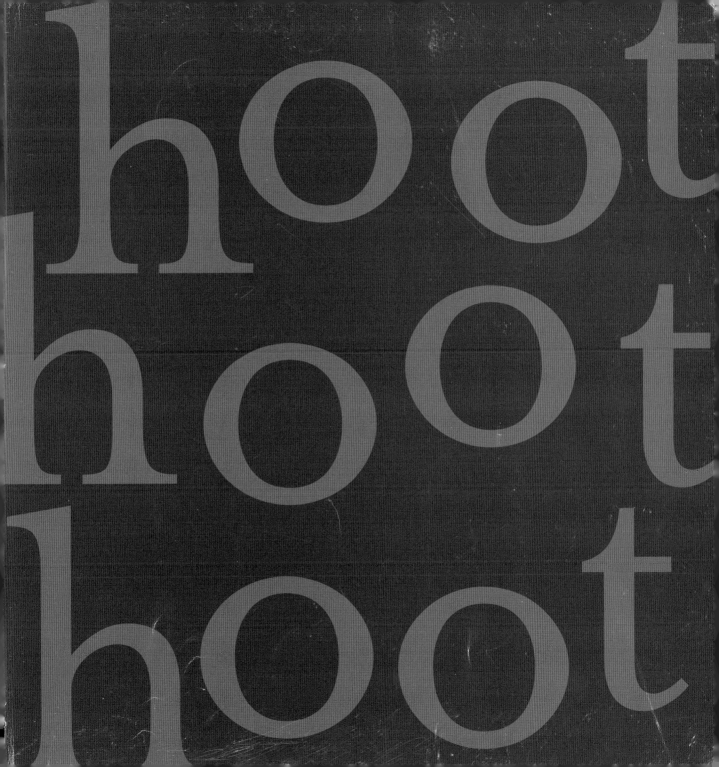